Usborne
Stories
to
Read Aloud

Usborne
Stories
to
Read Aloud

Retold by Felicity Brooks

Illustrated by Richard Johnson

CONTENTS

STORIES TO READ ALOUD

Some of these well-loved tales have been around for centuries, handed down by storytellers from one generation to the next, so no-one knows exactly where they came from. Others can be traced back to specific writers such as Hans Christian Andersen or the Brothers Grimm who listened to storytellers, wrote the tales down and published collections of them. Two of the stories here are from Aesop whose fables have been popular since he first told them in Ancient Greece more than two thousand years ago.

Aesop's stories always have a moral or lesson at the end, and many other tales may have remained popular because they teach us something about the world. We find out what can happen if we are too greedy, boastful, nosy, or just plain naughty; or we may see what the rewards are for being clever, resourceful, persevering, helpful, kind, or brave. Some tales stay popular simply because they are just slightly – and delightfully – scary.

It is probably for these reasons that similar tales occur all over the world. Often, different countries tell different versions of the same basic story, adding their own twist. For example, the 'magic' stone in 'Stone Soup' is sometimes a nail or sometimes a button; Little Red Riding Hood can trace her origins back to the Middle East or to Ancient China; 'Jack and the Beanstalk' is believed to have sailed to England with the Vikings to meet the giant-slayers of Celtic folklore.

So, turn the page to enter a wonderful world of big bad wolves, fishes that grant wishes, helpful little elves, talking bears, boastful hares, real princesses, boy-eating giants, and a runaway gingerbread man.

I hope you have as much fun reading these beautifully illustrated tales to your children as I have had retelling them.

Felicity Brooks

STONE SOUP

Many, many years ago, times were hard and a kind old man found himself wandering along a beach wondering where he could find his next meal. All he had left in the world were the clothes he stood up in, a friendly dog named Lucky and a large iron cooking pot.

"Well that's pretty!" he said to Lucky, bending down to pick up a shiny pebble from the shore. It was then he had an idea.

He put the stone in his pocket, picked up his pot and lugged it up the hill towards a small village.

There he found the village pump, filled the pot with water, heaved it over to the middle of the square and began to look for some sticks to make a fire.

All around, doors and windows were slamming shut and mothers were calling to their children to come in from the street. The old man and his dog were strangers in this village.

But one woman, who was on her way back from the market, wasn't scared.

"What are you up to?" she asked, putting down her basket of vegetables and peering into the pot.

"Oh, just making some stone soup," said the old man. "If you stay around, I'll show you the recipe. It's really delicious."

By now the water was beginning to bubble.

"First I add this special stone," said the old man, bringing the pretty pebble out of his pocket with a flourish and dropping it into the steaming water.

'Plop'

"Hmmm, smells good already," he said. "But, when you make stone soup, you must stir it well. I don't suppose you have a–?"

"Spoon? Oh, of course," said the woman eagerly and she popped into her cottage and came back with a big wooden spoon.

"That's very good," declared the old man loudly, slurping some soup from the spoon, "though I think a couple of onions would help improve it."

"Will these do?" asked the woman, taking two big onions from her basket.

"Well, let's see," said the old man, holding the onions up to inspect them.

"They might work," he said, eyeing her basket of vegetables, "but only if we could chop them finely and somehow mingle them with some carrots."

"Oh, I can do that," said the woman, and she popped back into her cottage for a knife and chopping board.

'Plop, plop, plop, plop'

"Now, that's more like it," said the old man, tasting the soup when the onions and carrots had cooked for a while. "But as we're near the sea, I think something like some fish or a crab would really help to bring out the taste of the stone."

By this time a few other villagers had gathered around, drawn by the cooking smell and the chatter of the old man, curious to see what he was doing.

"I never realized you could put crab in stone soup," said a young fisherman. "That's so lucky – I've got a couple here."

The old man watched patiently as the fisherman expertly cracked open the crabs, picked them clean of their meat with his pocketknife and added the meat to the pot.

'*Plop, plop, plop, plop*'

"What about these?" offered a young woman, holding out an apronful of potatoes. "I grew them in my garden. Do you think they would work in stone soup? I've got a bulb of fresh garlic that might be good, too."

"Well, I'm prepared to give them a try," said the old man. "It's not my usual recipe, but you never know . . . oh dear, the fire seems to be dying down."

While the young woman peeled and sliced the potatoes and garlic, the other villagers scurried around gathering more firewood to keep the pot simmering.

'*Plop, plop, plop, plop*'

"Let's see if it's ready," said the old man, dipping the spoon into the soup.

"Oh no!" he said, making a disappointed face. "This is a disaster! I completely forgot about the seasoning. The whole thing could be ruined."

"Don't worry," said the first woman. "I've got sea salt and pepper and some nice fresh herbs at home. I won't be a second!"

With the soup seasoned, the old man dipped the spoon into the soup again. He made a big show of blowing on the bubbling broth, shutting his eyes, slipping the soup slowly into his mouth and swallowing with a great gulp.

A huge grin spread across his face from ear to ear.

"PERFECT!" he cried and he punched the air in triumph.

"WOOF, WOOF, WOOF!" added Lucky, woken from his snooze by the shouting.

"Would anyone like to try some?" asked the old man.

"Yes, please!" said the young woman and she scuttled off to find some bowls and spoons and cups. Soon everyone was sitting in the village square, enjoying the stone soup.

"My word, this is delicious," said one villager.

"The best soup I've ever tasted," said another.

"That stone must be magic!" whispered a third. "Do you think he would sell it to us?"

But when the soup was finished, the old man washed out the pot, put the stone back into his pocket, called to Lucky and went on his way.

And for many years afterwards the villagers told tales about the kind and generous stranger who arrived mysteriously one evening and made stone soup for everyone in the village, before disappearing into the night followed by a small, friendly dog.

THE GINGERBREAD MAN

Once upon a time a little old man and a little old woman lived in a little old cottage near a big wide river. Most days they were happy taking care of their chickens and going for picnics on the riverbank. But once in a while, something made them sad, and that was the fact they had no children.

On one such morning, to cheer herself up, the little old woman decided to do some baking.

She mixed together butter, flour, eggs, molasses and a few pinches of ground ginger to make some dough. She rolled it out on her kitchen table with her heavy rolling pin, then cut out the shape of a little man.

With the point of her knife she made a half circle for his mouth and added two little currants for eyes, and three for buttons.

And the gingerbread man was done.

She put the little man into the oven and sat down at the table, waiting patiently for him to be ready. Soon the kitchen was filled with sweet, spicy baking smells.

"Mmmm," said her husband, wandering in from the garden. "That smells really–"

Just then there was a TAP, TAP, TAP on the oven door.

"Let me out!" called a little voice. "I don't want to burn!"
The little old woman bustled over and opened the oven door
a crack, but jumped back in surprise when out popped the
gingerbread man!

She was even more amazed when the little man raced across
the floor and dashed out of the door.

"Come back!" called the startled old woman.

"Come back here!" called the
little old man.
     But the gingerbread
man ran down the path
and out through the
gate, singing,

"Run! Run! As fast as you can.
You can't catch me,
I'm the gingerbread man!"

He ran along a track past
fields of cows and horses.

"Come back!" mooed a cow.
"We want to eat y-o-o-o-o-u!"
"Come here!" neighed a horse. "We're hungry!"

But the gingerbread man just ran and ran, singing, "I've run
away from a little old woman and a little old man and I can run
away from you too, yes I can!" and,

"Run! Run! As fast as you can.
You can't catch me,
I'm the gingerbread man!"

He sprinted past a farmer working in his fields.
"Come back here, young man!" called the farmer, dropping
his pitchfork in surprise. "I want to eat you."

But the gingerbread man kept on running, singing, "I've run away from a cow and a horse and a little old woman and a little old man and I can run away from you too, yes I can!" and,

"Run! Run! As fast as you can.
You can't catch me,
I'm the gingerbread man!"

He shot past a field of sheep.
"Stop!" baaed the sheep.
"Come b-a-a-a-ck here!
We want to eat you."

But the gingerbread
man ran on down the track
singing at the top of his voice, "I've run away from a farmer, a cow and a horse, a little old woman and a little old man and I can run away from you too, yes I can!" and,

"Run! Run! As fast as you can.
You can't catch me,
I'm the gingerbread man!"

By now, everyone was
chasing the gingerbread
man, but he was so quick
they were trailing some
way behind.

But then he had to stop.

He had reached the bank
of the big, wide river and
could run no further.

If he got wet, he'd start
to crumble, but he had to
find a way across before
the mooing, neighing,
baaing, shouting crowd
caught him and gobbled
him up.

That moment he glimpsed a long orange nose poking out of the reeds and a large fox slinking slowly towards him, sniffing the air.

"Can I help you, my tasty– er, I mean hasty friend?" asked the cunning fox.

"I – I – I can't get across the river," puffed the gingerbread man.

"Well, I can swim extremely well," said the sneaky fox, licking his leathery lips. "If you climb up onto my tail, I'll take you over in no time."

"Oh, thank you!" said the gingerbread man, and he grabbed hold of the fox's bushy tail and hauled himself up.

The fox plunged into the muddy water and began to paddle across. The gingerbread man clung to the soggy tail but the water started to drag it down.

"Oh, I'm sorry," said the fox. "My tail is sinking. You'll be so much safer on my back."

Very carefully, the gingerbread man crawled onto the fox's back, but soon the water was creeping up towards his feet.

"Oh, I'm so sorry," said the fox, "but my back's getting soggy. You'll be much, much safer on my nose."

Scared that he might soon start to crumble, the gingerbread man scrambled quickly up the fox's neck, between his ears and balanced on his long, silky snout.

"I'm so, so sorry about this," said the fox.

Then he flung back his head and flipped the gingerbread man into the air.

"SNAP!" went the fox's jaws and the gingerbread man was a quarter munched.

"SNAP!" went the fox again and the gingerbread man was half munched.

"SNAP, CRUNCH, SLURP!" went the fox and the gingerbread man was three-quarters munched.

"GULP," went the fox with a greedy grin.

And the gingerbread man was gone.

THE PRINCESS AND THE PEA

There was once a charming, handsome prince who had everything that anyone could possibly wish for in the world – fine clothes, oodles of gold, a thousand solid silver goblets, three pet rabbits, a stable full of horses, and a palace full of servants who swept and scrubbed and cooked and cleaned so he never had to lift a finger.

But this prince was never, ever happy.

Because he longed to marry a real princess, but he just couldn't find one.

He'd ridden far and wide over the country and sailed across every sea and ocean in search of a real princess. He'd met girls from every land – funny ones and clever ones, tall ones and short ones, sporty ones and dainty ones, and one with enormous feet. But somehow he never found the real princess he was looking for.

So he returned home to live a lonely life with only his parents, the king and queen, to keep him company.

"You're not getting any younger," his mother liked to remind him. "You really *must* find a real princess who wants to be your wife soon or we won't have any grandchildren!"

"I know," said the prince sadly, "and I'm doing my best, but I don't think there are any *real* princesses left for me to meet."

*   *   *

One evening the prince was sitting forlornly by the fire with his head in his hands. He'd almost given up hope of ever finding *anyone* to fall in love with, let alone a real princess. Outside, a terrible storm was raging. Wind was howling around the turrets, rain was lashing the windows and lightning ripped through the sky. Then there was another sound.

'Tap, tap, tap'

"What was that?" said the queen.

"Someone at the door?" said the king.

"I'll go," said the prince and he plodded over to unbolt the heavy oak door.

"Oh goodness!" said the prince. "It's a girl! A real, live girl!"

"Who looks like a drowned rat," added the queen.

"Sorry to ask," said the stranger, rain streaming down her face, "but I'm a terribly long way from home. This storm is awful and I'm completely drenched. I don't suppose it would be possible to stay here for the night?"

"Of course," said the prince without a moment's hesitation. "Come in and dry yourself by the fire."

The girl sloshed through the door and squelched over to the fire. Water dripped from her cloak and made a puddle on the floor. When she pulled down her hood, the prince couldn't help noticing a small tiara glinting in the firelight.

"Sorry to ask," said the prince shyly, staring at her soggy feet, "but I don't suppose you happen to be a princess?"

"Of course," said the princess. "I was just on the way back to my palace and I got caught in this terrible storm. Oh dear! I'm making such a mess of your rug."

The queen's ears pricked up when she heard the word 'princess' and she trotted off to instruct the servants to take care of the visitor. For the rest of the evening, while the prince and princess sat talking and laughing by the fire, servants scurried in and out with warm towels, hot drinks and fine food.

But the queen was nowhere to be seen. She was upstairs in one of the bedrooms hatching a plan.

"We'll soon find out if that bedraggled girl is a real princess," she said to the housekeeper. "Now bring me every mattress you can find. I need at least twenty."

"And a pea!" she called to the maid. "Get me a dried pea from the kitchen. I need one for our guest's special bed."

The queen slipped the pea under a sheet on the bed then told the servants to pile up all the mattresses on top.

The maid and housekeeper shot each other quizzical looks, thinking the queen must be going a little crazy, but they did as they were told.

"Now all we need is a ladder," said the queen finally.
"Um, yes, of course, Your Majesty," said the maid.

*   *   *

When it was time for bed, the housekeeper came to show the visitor up to her room.

"I've had a wonderful evening," the princess said.
"Me too," said the prince with a dreamy smile on his face.

The princess was a little confused when she saw the twenty mattresses and the ladder in her bedroom, but she was far too polite to say anything.

So she climbed dutifully up to the top of the mountain of mattresses to get into bed and tried to fall fast asleep.

In the morning the princess staggered down to breakfast looking tired and grumpy.

"Did you sleep well, my dear?" asked the king.

"Of course not!" blurted out the princess. "I had a terrible night. I just couldn't get comfortable because there was a huge lump in the mattresses!"

"I knew it!" declared the queen delightedly. "I knew you must be a real princess!"

The visitor looked puzzled.

"Only a real princess can feel a pea through twenty mattresses," laughed the queen.

"At last!" cried the prince joyfully. "Will you marry me?"

"Of course," said the princess.

And so they were married and lived happily ever after, and the famous pea was placed on a velvet cushion in the palace museum. It may still be there today (if no one has eaten it, of course).

THE BOY WHO CRIED WOLF

"I am *so* bored," thought Owen the shepherd boy.
"All I do every day is sit on this tree stump,
on this hillside, and watch these sheep.
All day and every day, always the same.
I wish something exciting would happen."

He gazed down to the village where he lived. Smoke curled up lazily from the chimneys into a hazy sky. A dog barked and somewhere a baby was crying. Nothing exciting there.

He looked back at his flock grazing on the rough grass.

"Baaa!" said one of the sheep.

"Baaaaa to you!" said Owen, just to have someone to talk to.

It was then he had an idea to stir things up. If nothing exciting ever happened, he would make something happen. Even if it was a little naughty . . .

Owen stood up, jumped on top of his tree stump, took a very deep breath, cupped his hands around his mouth and shouted as loud as he possibly could:

"WOLF! WOLF!

There's a wolf attacking the sheep!

HELP! HELP! HELP!"

His cries echoed around the valley and down into the village, and soon he could see people armed with sticks, pitchforks and shovels scrambling up the steep path towards the field.

Young men and women took the lead. Older people puffed along behind.

"WOLF! WOLF!" shouted Owen over and over again.

The startled sheep flocked into the far corner of the field as the villagers charged towards them.

"Where's the wolf?" demanded one man urgently.

"Where . . . where is it, boy?" panted another.

"I can't see it," said a red-faced man.

Owen just burst into laughter.

"Tricked you!" he called. "No wolf today!"

"Idiot!" said the red-faced man, thumping his stick on the ground.

"You silly boy," said another, flopping down on the grass.

"We dropped EVERYTHING for this, and you've wasted ALL our time!" shouted a tall woman, gathering up her skirts and striding angrily off down the hillside.

Strangely, none of the villagers seemed to see the funny side of Owen's little trick. And they were even less happy when he did exactly the same thing a couple of weeks later . . . and a week after that.

The third time when Owen cried "WOLF!" not quite as many people turned up. Those who did were furious when they realized they had been tricked yet again. But Owen really didn't care. He loved playing tricks on people, and boredom always seemed to get the better of him, despite all the lectures he got from his mother.

*   *   *

Early one misty morning, some months later, Owen was once again sitting on his tree stump when he saw a large furry shape emerge from the forest on the far side of the field. It had big pointed ears, sharp white teeth and a long bushy tail. This time it really was a . . .

"WOLF! WOLF!" shouted Owen in a terrified voice. "HELP! HELP! There's a wolf!"

His shouts echoed around the valley and down to the village.

"Just listen to that silly boy trying to trick us again," the tall woman said to her friend as they were heaving water from the well.

"He must think we were born yesterday. I'm not falling for it this time," said the friend.

"Me neither," called her red-faced husband, who was up on a ladder repairing the roof of their cottage.

Only Owen's mother abandoned her chores and plodded dutifully up the hillside, ready to give her son the most mighty scolding. But by the time she got there, Owen had stopped shouting. She found him sitting on the ground with his head in his hands, sobbing pitifully.

The wolf was nowhere to be seen. And all the sheep were dead.

And the lesson of the story?

If you tell lies, no one believes you when you are telling the truth.

GOLDILOCKS AND THE THREE BEARS

If, one day, you follow a narrow, winding path into the Deep Dark Forest, you might come across a grassy clearing and find the little house where the three bears live. But if it's early in the morning when you get there, the bears won't be at home.

Because every day Father Bear, Mother Bear and Baby Bear make some porridge for their breakfast then go for a walk in the forest while they wait for it to cool.

Indeed, the three bears were out enjoying their stroll on the morning that a rather nosy little girl named Goldilocks followed that winding path and stumbled across their house.

"I wonder who lives here?" she said to herself, pushing on the wooden door, which swung open with a loud creak.

"Hello!" called Goldilocks as she wandered into the kitchen. "Anyone at home?"

On the table, she saw three bowls of porridge. "Mmmm," she murmured hungrily.

Without thinking twice, she picked up a spoon and tried the porridge in the biggest bowl.

"Too hot!" she said.

Next she tried the porridge in the middle-sized bowl.

"Too cold!" she said and threw down the spoon and bowl in disgust. The cold porridge splattered all over the table and walls.

Finally, she tasted the porridge in the smallest bowl.

"Just right!" she said, and she ate it all up, every last spoonful, and even licked the bowl.

"I need to sit down after all that porridge," thought Goldilocks. She wandered into another room and saw three wooden chairs in front of a fire.

She climbed up on the biggest chair first.

"Too high!" she said and jumped down again.

Next she tried the middle-sized chair.

"Too uncomfortable!" she said, and went to try the smallest chair instead.

"Just right!" said Goldilocks, but just at that moment she heard a very loud

'CRACK!'

. . . as the chair broke into pieces.

"Ohhhhh dear!" giggled Goldilocks, and she kicked the pieces into a pile by the wall, hoping no one would notice.

Looking around, she spotted a staircase in the corner of the room and decided to explore upstairs. In the bedroom, she found three comfy-looking beds.

"Ahhhh," she yawned. She was starting to feel sleepy.

She jumped onto the biggest bed, wiggled around and messed up the sheets as she tried to get comfortable.

"Too hard!" she said.

The middle-sized bed looked very inviting, but when she climbed onto it, it almost swallowed her up.

"Too soft!" said Goldilocks. She threw off the covers, eased herself out and went to try the smallest bed instead.

"Just right," sighed Goldilocks happily and she snuggled down for a little nap.

*   *   *

"I'm hungry!" said Baby Bear as the bear family reached the grassy clearing at the end of their walk.

"Almost home," said Mother Bear. But at that moment, she noticed that the door of their house was swinging open in the breeze. She started running across the grass.

"Someone's been eating MY porridge!" growled Father Bear, storming into the kitchen just behind her.

"Someone's been eating MY porridge, too!" said Mother Bear. "And look at the awful mess they've made in my kitchen!"

Baby Bear stared into his bowl and wailed.

"Someone's been eating MY porridge, too, and they've eaten it all up!"

The three bears rushed into the living room.

"Someone's been sitting in MY chair," snarled Father.

"Someone's been sitting in MY chair, too," roared Mother.

"Someone's been sitting in m-m-m-my little chair," sobbed Baby Bear, "and now it's all broken. WAAAAAAAH!"

The furious bears stomped upstairs and saw that their beds were covered in crumpled sheets and blankets.

"Someone's been sleeping in MY bed!" bellowed Father.

"Someone's been sleeping in MY bed, too," yelled Mother.

"Someone's been sleeping in MY bed," bawled Baby Bear, "and she's still here!"

Goldilocks's eyes snapped open to see three angry bears standing over her, roaring and growling and yelling and shouting.

Their sharp teeth glistened and she could feel their hot breath on her face. She had never had such a shock in her life.

Goldilocks screamed loudly, jumped out of bed, scrambled down the stairs and raced out of the house. She ran and ran and ran, across the grassy clearing, back along the winding path, out of the Deep Dark Forest and all the way home.

And she never, ever, EVER went into that forest again.

LITTLE RED RIDING HOOD

Some children can't be parted from their teddy bears, and some cling to their baby blankets, but there was once a little girl who was different. She would never go anywhere without her red velvet cloak. In fact she wore it so often that people began calling her 'Little Red Riding Hood'. And the name soon stuck.

"You're not wearing that *again,* are you?" sighed Red Riding Hood's mother one morning when the little girl skipped into the kitchen wearing the bright red cloak.

"Of course I am!" laughed Red Riding Hood. "No one would recognize me if I wore something else."

"Well, it's good you're ready to go out," said her mother. "You need to be very helpful this morning and walk through the forest to Grandma's house. She's not at all well, you see, and a visit from you would really cheer her up."

"Oh, and take this," added her mother, thrusting a basket of cakes into Red Riding Hood's hands.

"But I thought I wasn't allowed to walk through the forest by myself," said Red Riding Hood. "What about the Big Bad W–"

"Oh stuff and nonsense!" declared her mother breezily, holding open the door. "I'm sure that's just silly stories. You'll be fine if you stick to the path. I've been through the forest a hundred times and never ever met the Big Bad–"

"HOOOOOOWL!" came a noise from the forest.

"What was that?" asked Red Riding Hood.

"Just a friendly owl, I expect," said her mother. "Bye now!"

Little Red Riding Hood pulled her hood up over her head and set off along the path towards her grandmother's house, clutching the basket and singing softly to herself.

It was a fine morning and the forest was full of chirping birds and spring flowers. She could hear in the distance the dull thudding sound of a woodcutter chopping away at a tree trunk.

The little girl felt very grown up being out in the forest by herself. She loved hearing the wind in the treetops and seeing small birds darting in and out of the bushes. What she didn't notice was a large dark shape slinking slowly through the undergrowth towards her.

"Good morning!" growled the large dark shape, jumping out in front of her and blocking her path.

"Oh, g-g-good morning," stuttered Little Red Riding Hood, quite shocked that a wolf was talking to her.

"And where are you off to this fine morning, young lady?" asked the wolf cheerily.

"I'm just on my way to my grandmother's house," blurted out Red Riding Hood. "She's not at all well, you see, and I'm taking her some cakes."

"Oh," said the wolf. "That's very kind of you. And where does your grandmother live? Is it far?"

"Not really," said Red Riding Hood, still not quite believing she was chatting with a wolf. "She lives on the other side of the forest. You just stick to this path and it's the first cottage on the right. Um . . . I hope you don't mind me asking," she continued, "but you don't happen to be the Big Bad–"

"Oh, no, no, no," interrupted the wolf. "That's my very distant cousin, Boris. Gives us all a big, bad name! I'm much more your small, good wolf type. I like picking wildflowers, and, um . . . " He glanced quickly at the basket. "And baking."

"That's lucky," said Red Riding Hood, "as I'd hate to meet the Big Bad Wolf!"

"Oh, no chance of that around here," laughed the wolf, revealing his sharp white fangs dripping with saliva.

"Listen, my dear," he said. "I have a splendid idea – why don't you pick some pretty flowers for your grandmother? I'm sure she'd like that. I happen to know there's a lovely patch of primroses just over there behind those oak trees." He gestured vaguely off into the forest.

"Good idea!" said Red Riding Hood. "Bye!" And she skipped off the path and disappeared among the trees.

*   *   *

Now that wolf was a liar (as I am sure you have already guessed) and as soon as Little Red Riding Hood was out of sight, he ran as fast as he could all the way to her grandmother's house and knocked on the door.

"Hello, Granny!" he called squeakily, trying his best to sound like a little girl.

"Is that you, Red Riding Hood?" Grandmother called back.

"Oh yes, Granny," squeaked the wolf. "I have some delicious cakes for you."

"Let yourself in, dear," called Grandmother weakly from her bed. "The door's not locked."

"Yes, Granny," said the wolf. "Here I come . . ."

Sad to say, but Grandmother was so thin and frail that the Big Bad Wolf swallowed her up in one greedy gulp.

Then he put on one of her nightdresses, pulled a nightcap over his ears, wrapped himself in Grandma's shawl and perched her glasses on the end on his long snout.

The wolf snuggled down under the covers of Grandmother's bed and waited for Red Riding Hood to arrive.

When Red Riding Hood found her way to the cottage a little while later, she was surprised to see the door swinging open.

"Grandmother!" she called up the stairs. "It's me, Red Riding Hood. Are you awake? I've brought you some cakes."

"Oh, thank you, dear," called the wolf, muffling his voice with the edge of a blanket. "I have such a bad cold and my throat is so sore. Come up here, dear. I'm too weak to get out of bed."

Red Riding Hood bounded up the stairs.

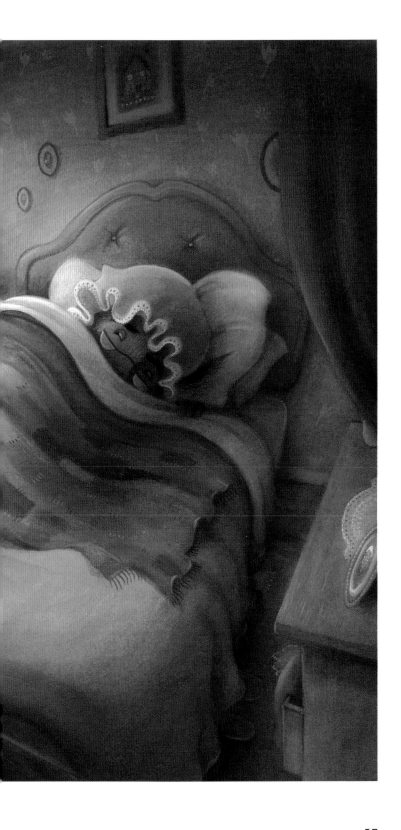

Grandmother was
huddled up under a pile
of blankets with just
her head poking out.
She looked very strange.

Red Riding Hood
put down her basket
and flowers and went to
sit on the end of the bed.

"Poor Granny," she
said. "You really don't
look yourself today.
What big ears you have!"
"All the better to
hear you with, my dear,"
replied the wolf.
"And what big eyes
you have," said Red
Riding Hood, moving
a little closer.

"All the better to see you with," said the wolf.

"And what huge, hairy arms you have, Granny," said the girl.

"All the better to hug you with, dear," said the wolf, stretching out his paws towards her.

"And what big teeth you have!" said Red Riding Hood.

"All the better to EAT YOU WITH!" snarled the wolf, and he leaped out of bed, pounced on Red Riding Hood and swallowed her whole.

"Well, hello dear," said Grandmother inside the wolf's belly. "We're in a bit of a pickle, aren't we?"

"Help!" called Red Riding Hood as loudly as she could. "We're inside the Big Bad Wolf!

H-E-L-P!"

After his enormous meal, the wolf burped loudly, scratched his ears and stretched out on the bed. He was soon fast asleep and snoring noisily.

Now, it just so happened that a woodcutter had to pass Grandmother's cottage on his way home from the forest. When he saw the door swinging open and heard the terrible snoring and dull cries, he decided to see if Grandmother was alright.

As soon as he saw the wolf's big belly bulging under the covers, the woodcutter realized what had happened.

He grabbed Grandmother's sewing scissors and with a quick 'snip, snip, snip' opened up the wolf's belly and heaved Red Riding Hood and Grandmother out.

"Gosh, it was dark in there!" said Red Riding Hood, blinking in the daylight.

"And very hot, too!" added Grandmother, picking up her fan to cool herself down.

The wolf was still sleeping soundly while they came up with a clever plan. He didn't even stir when they stuffed his belly with stones from the garden. And he was still snoring away when Grandmother sewed it up neatly with her strongest

"That will teach this naughty wolf not to go around eating old ladies!" she said, snipping off the last bit of thread. "Now, how about a nice cup of tea and some cake?"

*　　　*　　　*

And indeed that Big Bad Wolf had to change his ways.

With the stones clattering around inside him wherever he went, he could no longer sneak around scaring young girls or gobbling up grandmothers. So he spent his days gathering nuts and berries, picking wildflowers and baking cakes.

And as for Little Red Riding Hood?

Well, she learned that wolves are not always who they say they are, and she never got tricked by a Big Bad Wolf again.

THE GOLDEN FISH

An old fisherman and his wife lived in a tiny tumbledown hut by the shores of a beautiful lake. They were extremely poor, but they always had fresh fish to eat, and sometimes even enough left over to sell in the market.

But, however many fish the old man caught, and however hard he worked, his wife was never happy.

"Oh, just look at this awful old tumbledown hut with its leaky roof," she moaned. "And I'm so, *so* sick of wearing this horrible shabby dress. If only I had married a handsome prince, I'd live in a palace and have wonderful sparkly dresses!"

Even though she was always unhappy, the old man loved his wife very much and did everything he could to try to please her. One morning, as usual, he dragged his scruffy old boat through the rain, down to the water's edge and rowed out to the middle of the lake to start fishing.

"Maybe this will be my lucky day," he thought as he cast his net out into the green water on the end of a long, scratchy rope. "Maybe I'll catch so many fish, we'll have enough money to buy a new boat and fix the roof of the hut."

While the old man daydreamed, raindrops plopped into the water around him. The boat rocked lazily and the water lapped gently against its sides.

Splish, splash, splish, splash, splish, splash.

"And we could buy some fresh bread and some cheese in the market and some creamy milk . . ."

Splish, splash, splish, splash, splish, splash.

"And my wife will smile and clap her hands when I show her the gorgeous new dress I have bought her . . ."

Splish, splash, splish, splash, splish, SPLASH!

A sudden sharp tug on the rope jolted the old man out of his daydream.

"What on earth . . ." he muttered, bracing himself against the side of the boat with his legs to begin hauling up the net. Whatever was inside it felt bigger and heavier than anything he had ever caught before.

Hand over hand, he started to pull up the rope, straining and puffing to land the enormous catch.

"New roof – new boat – new dress," he chanted. The net seemed to get heavier and heavier every time he heaved. "Fresh cheese, fresh milk, FRESH BREAD!" he shouted gleefully as at last the net emerged from the depths.

With a final great groan, he hauled the net over the side. It landed in the bottom of the boat with a . . . *plop!*

The old man fell back in confusion, caught his breath, then launched himself forward and started scrabbling frantically around with his hands. After all that heaving, and all that hoping, his dreams were dashed. The net was completely empty!

Then he heard a strange little voice.

"Help me! Please, help me!"

It seemed to be coming from somewhere inside the net. When he scrabbled around again, right at the bottom he found a tiny, golden fish, gasping out the words in a human voice.

"If you let me go, I'll grant you three wishes," said the fish.

"I'm a magic fish, honest, Mister! They call me the Wish Fish. That's why I can talk . . . and do this."

To prove its point, the fish flapped free of the net, jumped up in the air and turned a fancy somersault before flopping back down at the old man's feet.

"Ta dah!" gasped the fish, clapping its fins together.

The old man just stared, open-mouthed, unable to believe what he was hearing or seeing. Then, in shock, he blurted out the first thing he could think of:

"A roof, please! A new roof. That's what I wish for. A roof that doesn't leak."

"No sooner said than done," said the fish. "Do you like that? *No sooner said than done!* A famous old genie taught me to say that at wish school."

"Um, yes," said the old man.
"All right, Mister. A new roof it is," said the fish. Then it

jumped up and over the side of the boat, plopped into the water and disappeared into the murky green depths.

*   *   *

The old man lost no time in rowing back to tell his wife about what had happened. But when he neared the shore, he saw she was already running down to meet him, waving and pointing towards their hut.

"You'll never guess what," she gabbled. "Pouring with rain, but it's fixed. Our roof! It's fixed! Doesn't leak! Looks like new! No idea how!"

"I do," said the old man.

When he explained all about the fish and the wishes, far from being happy, the old man's wife looked close to tears.

"Is that all you could think of?" she moaned. "Fix an old roof? We hardly have a crust of bread to eat or a stitch to wear, and all you could wish for was that!"

The old man just sighed.

"Go back and ask that fish for something else," his wife demanded. "Quickly, while it's still in the mood to grant wishes."

So the fisherman rowed back out to the middle of the lake and called: "Here, wishy fishy! Here, little fish! Please come back!"

Seconds later the fish popped its head above the water. "Happy with your roof?" it asked.

"Oh, yes, lovely job, thank you. Beautiful workmanship and all that, but my wife would like something . . . something more."

"More?" said the fish. "MORE! Yes, well, alright. Whatever the Missus wants."

"A new . . . a new house?" asked the fisherman hesitantly.

"No sooner said than done," said the fish and vanished once more into the depths of the lake.

And so the fisherman and his wife got a splendid new house, with shiny new furniture, soft beds, a wardrobe full of gorgeous dresses and a kitchen stocked with fantastic food.

But still the fisherman's wife wanted more.

"I'd like to be queen," she declared. "Then I could rule over all the people and all the land. I'd ride around in a golden carriage, wear a golden crown and everyone would have to curtsey and bow to me. Now that would really make me happy."

The third time the fisherman rowed out to call to the fish, he had a funny feeling in his stomach. What if the fish couldn't grant that wish? What would his wife say?

But the fish appeared, as before,
and happily granted the third wish.
And when the fisherman returned to
the shore, he saw his wife waving to him
through the window of a sparkling carriage
drawn by six white horses. Their splendid
new house was now an immense
palace with turrets and guards,
and servants running
this way and that.

The fisherman sighed. "I miss the old days," he thought.
"But at least my wife is happy at last."

Sadly, he was wrong.

"I want to rule EVERYTHING!" the queen announced that evening. "I want to rule ALL the animals and ALL the fish in ALL the lakes and ALL the seas and ALL the oceans in ALL the world. And I want it NOW!"

"But . . . " said the fisherman, remembering that they'd used up all three wishes.

"Go and tell that fish what I want," said his wife, gesturing with her hand for him to leave. "I COMMAND YOU!"

With a heavy heart, once more the fisherman rowed out to the middle of the lake in his scruffy old boat.

"Wishy fishy!" he called quietly.

"Oh, whatever is it now?" said the fish grumpily, popping up beside the boat. "Is the Missus still not happy?"

"No," said the old man. "She still wants more. She wants . . ."

"Too greedy!" said the fish, not even waiting to hear what she wanted. "Goodbye!" and with a flick of its little tail, it disappeared into the deep, green water.

The fisherman turned his boat and began to row slowly back towards the shore, slowly back to his tumbledown hut with its leaky roof, and slowly back to his wife in her shabby old dress.

THE HARE AND THE TORTOISE

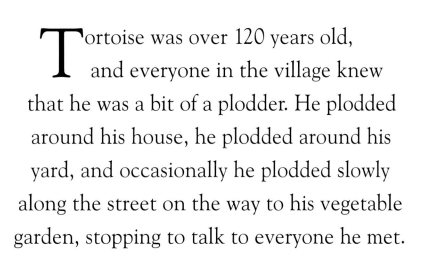

Tortoise was over 120 years old, and everyone in the village knew that he was a bit of a plodder. He plodded around his house, he plodded around his yard, and occasionally he plodded slowly along the street on the way to his vegetable garden, stopping to talk to everyone he met.

"Good morning, Mrs. Badger. How are your little ones today?" he would ask, or, "Hello Mr. Fox. Sorry to hear Mrs. Fox isn't feeling well. Anything I can do to help?"

And when Tortoise wasn't plodding around, he liked nothing more than to sit in his front yard watching the world go by, waving cheerfully and chatting with the animals that passed.

"Lovely morning, little bunnies!" he'd call. "Don't forget to stop by for some juicy lettuce leaves on your way back."

So, although he was a bit of an old plodder, Tortoise was very well liked. He always had time for other animals, and he had plenty of friends. Not like young Hare.

Hare was fast. Hare loved to run. He dashed here and there. He raced up roads. He rushed over rivers. He darted in and out of doors and he hared up hills. Hare never stopped. He was the fastest animal in the village. And didn't he know it!

"Morning, dawdler!" he called each Monday when he sprinted past Tortoise's yard. "Can't stop!" And then he'd hurtle up the hill and disappear in a cloud of dust.

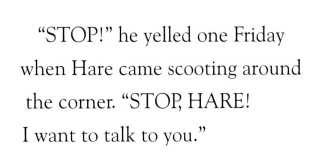

And so it went on:

"Hello, lazybones!" on Tuesday.

"Morning, Grandpa!" on Wednesday.

"Hello, you old plodder!" on Thursday.

Until one day Tortoise had had enough.

"STOP!" he yelled one Friday
when Hare came scooting around
the corner. "STOP, HARE!
I want to talk to you."

Hare skidded to a surprised halt.

"What is it, old thing?" he asked. "Not got enough energy to
open your gate this morning? Need help lifting your own shell?"

"No, I've had an idea. You see I'm tired of your teasing, and
we're all sick of your boasting, so I'd like to challenge you to a race."

"What?" said Hare in disbelief. "*You* challenge *me?*"

"Yes," said Tortoise firmly. "Once around the village tomorrow.
Start at the old oak tree at nine."

"But everyone knows I'm the fastest runner in the village," said Hare. "It wouldn't be fair. I'd have to carry you home at midnight!" Hare burst into a fit of mocking laughter.

"All the same," said Tortoise slowly. "I'd like to try."

"Alright then, Grandpa," chuckled Hare. "Tomorrow at nine. May the fastest animal win!"

And with this he whizzed off up the hill, still laughing to himself at the very idea of racing Tortoise.

*   *   *

When Tortoise's friends heard about the race, they did all they could to try to stop it.

"You can't go racing around at your age," said Dog. "You'll kill yourself!"

"Well, I'm not backing out now," replied Tortoise stubbornly. "And somebody has to show that rude young Hare that speed isn't everything. Now, if you'll excuse me, I really need to get a good night's sleep."

In the morning, Tortoise set off at seven and plodded slowly up towards the old oak tree, enjoying the feeling of the sun on his shell and stopping, as usual, to chat with friends along the way.

As he approached the starting line, he was surprised to see almost the whole village gathered around the tree. The crowd gave a big cheer when they saw him trudging towards them.

"Morning, Lightning," teased Hare, who was already running up and down behind the start line and making a big show of stretching his legs.

"Good morning, young Hare," said Tortoise politely as he ambled up to the line. "Good morning, Mr. Owl. And thanks for being our referee. If I'm on my usual form, it'll be over in a flash!"

Owl laughed and got ready to start the race.
"On your marks, get set, GO!" he shouted.
The crowd cheered.

Hare shot off, bounding along the stony track. Very soon he was just a ball of dust in the distance.

Tortoise, meanwhile, inched over the
line, moving at his normal plodding pace
and carefully placing one foot in front of
the other in a steady rhythm.

Plod,   plod,   plod,   plod

Plod,   plod,   plod,   plod

"Slow and steady, here we go,"
he chanted to himself as he plodded
along the path with the cheers of
the crowd still ringing in his ears.

Plod,   plod,   plod,   plod

After half an hour, he finally
trudged out of sight over the brow of the hill.

Hare, meanwhile, was on the other side of the village,
pounding a path through the woods. Squawking birds flew up
into the air, alarmed at his approach.

Rabbits scurried into their burrows in fear of being mown down as he thundered through.

"Huh, this is not much of a race," thought Hare, hurdling a hedge. "That old Tortoise must be way behind by now."

The summer sun was getting hotter and hotter as it rose into a cloudless blue sky. Hare was getting very thirsty. He leaped high in the air over a small stream, landed with a loud thud and skidded to a sudden halt.

It was time for a drink.

Hare lay flat on his stomach, took a big gulp of the cool water, then plonked himself down on the grass in the shade of a tree, just off the main path.

"So much time," he thought, lying back and admiring the shapes of the leaves against the blue sky.
"I could quite easily walk backwards the rest of the way and that old plodder still wouldn't catch up with me. Think I might just take a little nap . . ."

When the rabbits finally
ventured back out of their
burrows, they saw that
Hare had fallen fast asleep.

*   *   *

"My feet hurt," thought
Tortoise, plodding along the path.

Plod,   plod,   plod,   plod

"And my bones ache."

Plod,   plod,   plod,   plod

"And the sun is so hot."

Plod,   plod,   plod,   plod

"And my shell is so heavy."

Plod,   plod,   plod,   plod

"I'd love to curl up inside it and have a nice little nap."
But Tortoise didn't stop.

He trudged past a henhouse.
"Go on, Tortoise!" clucked the hens.

He plodded on past Dog's house.
"Go on, my friend. You can do it!" shouted Dog.

He tramped past a flock of sheep.
"Baaaa," said the sheep (because that's all sheep can say).
"Thanks, my dear friends," panted Tortoise.

Plod,   plod,   plod,   plod

On and on and on he walked, step after weary step through
the heat of the afternoon. One foot in front of the other, again
and again and again and again.

At last he reached the welcome shade of the woods.

By now he was exhausted. His feet were so sore and he was so thirsty, it was a relief to wade through a cool stream and take a little sip of water.

"Oh my, oh my," he said out loud in the middle of the stream, stopping for just a moment to enjoy the feel of the water on his tired legs. "I'm really not sure I can keep going. This was a stupid idea!"

"You can do it, Tortoise!" said a little voice. A small bunny popped her head out of her burrow. "You can show that Hare!"

"He thinks he's *so* much better than us, just because he can run fast," said her sister.

"But *he* never gives us juicy lettuce leaves," said the first one. "Go on, Tortoise! We want you to win!"

"Well, um, I can only do my best," grunted Tortoise, hauling himself clumsily out of the water.

Tortoise took a deep breath. "Slow and steady, here we go," he chanted and set out on the last leg of the race.

Plod,   plod,   plod,   plod

Plod,   plod,   plod,   plod

When he finally cleared the woods, he could see, at last, the black shape of the oak tree against the setting sun. He thought he heard some faint cheers carried towards him on the wind.

"That Hare must have won hours ago," he sighed.
"What an old fool I am."

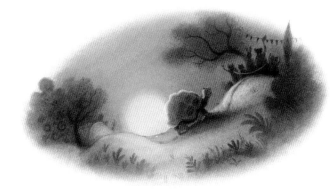

But Hare hadn't won. Hare was still dozing deep in the woods as the sun began to set.

It was the distant cheering and clapping of the animals urging Tortoise towards the finish line that finally woke him. Hare twitched back to life and jumped up in confusion.

"Where the… ? What the… ? Why's it dark? The race!" he cried, suddenly remembering.

Hare bounded off along the path towards the edge of the woods, racing faster than he had ever raced before. He tore down the track and out of the trees and quickly scanned the horizon for the old oak tree.

He couldn't believe what he saw.

There, far ahead of him, was the lumbering shape of that old plodding Tortoise tottering towards the finish line.

"N O O O O O O !" screamed Hare, taking one huge leap after another. Groaning with the enormous effort, he made one final, desperate dash for the finish.

But he was too late.

Plod,   plod,   plod,   PLOD.

"HURRAY!"

Tortoise staggered across the line to an enormous cheer from the crowd. Hare sprinted over two seconds later.

He stamped his feet, threw himself down in frustration and started wailing and hammering the ground with his fists.

Tortoise slowly lowered his heavy old shell onto the grass with a relieved sigh and put a comforting leg on Hare's shoulder.

"There, there, young man," he said in his soothing, croaky old voice. "It was only a race."

"But HOW?" sobbed Hare. "How d-d-did you win?"

"Slow and steady wins the race," said Tortoise with a smile.

THE ELVES AND THE SHOEMAKER

There was once a kindly shoemaker who lived with his wife Clara in a room above their shop. For many years, life was good. The shoemaker worked hard and the people of the town always came to his shop when they wanted a new pair of shoes. Until the day the Crafty Cobbler came to town.

The Crafty Cobbler wasn't a cobbler at all, and he certainly wasn't a craftsman. He didn't even know how to make shoes.

He just bought badly made shoes from other towns and sold them very cheaply.

Soon people were flocking to his shop. They liked the look of the cheap new shoes and they didn't know they would soon leak and fall apart.

It wasn't long before the kind shoemaker found he had few customers left, very little money, and only enough leather to make one pair of shoes.

"What are we going to do?" said Clara sadly. "With no shoes to sell and no customers, we'll be ruined."

"I don't know," sighed the shoemaker. "I've made shoes all my life, but that Crafty Cobbler has taken all our business and we can't even afford to buy more leather."

He was sitting hunched over his workbench as he had always done, carefully cutting out the leather pieces to make the last pair of shoes.

"We'll just have to see what happens," he said wearily. "Let's go to bed. I'll finish these in the morning."

*   *   *

The next morning, the shoemaker came down early. He hadn't slept well. He flung open the shutters, blinked in the daylight and rubbed his eyes. Then he gave a little gasp of surprise.

"What on earth? Look at this! SHOES!" he shouted.

Clara came running down the stairs to see her husband staring and pointing at his bench, mouth open in amazement.

There on the bench, gleaming in the early morning light, was the most perfect pair of shoes either of them had ever seen.

Utterly mystified, the shoemaker picked up one of the shoes and began to examine it.

"Just look at these stitches," he said.

"So tiny and neat," said Clara.

"And this buckle!" said the shoemaker.

"So shiny and bright," said Clara.

"It must be magic!" said the shoemaker.

"They're so perfect!" declared Clara. "And I bet they'll sell."

She carried the magic shoes over to the empty shop window and carefully placed them on a box in the middle.

Moments later, the shop door flew open and a well-dressed man strode in.

"How much are those shoes in the window?" he asked. "I really must have them! They are *just* what I need."

Within minutes he had tried on the shoes and dropped a silver coin into the shoemaker's hand.

"Keep the change!" he called as he made for the door.

"Maybe our luck is changing," said Clara cheerfully, closing the door behind him.

With the money from the shoes, the shoemaker was able to buy enough leather to make two more pairs, along with four shiny buckles. He spent the afternoon marking out the leather and cutting out the pieces, ready to start sewing the next day.

But, in the morning, there on the bench were two more pairs of perfect shoes, ready to go in the window.

"These are so much better than those shoddy shoes from up the road," said one of their old customers as he tried on a pair. "I bought some a month ago from the Crafty Cobbler and they've fallen to pieces already!"

"Well, you do have to pay a bit more for real craftsmanship!" said the shoemaker with a little smile.

With the money from selling the two pairs of shoes, the shoemaker could buy enough leather for four pairs, and, once again, four perfect pairs of shoes appeared, as if by magic, on his workbench overnight.

And so it went on.

Eight pairs . . .

Sixteen . . .

Thirty-two . . .

The shoemaker soon started cutting out patterns for fancy ladies' shoes, beautiful boots in the latest style, dainty slippers, children's sandals and sturdy walking boots.

And whatever he prepared, all the shoes and boots were always perfectly finished by the morning.

Business was booming. The shop window was full each day and usually empty by nightfall. Lines of customers began to form early in the morning with people eager to get hold of a pair of the beautiful shoes with perfect stitching.

"We'll soon be rich!" said Clara happily one evening, shutting the door after the final customer of the day.

"I've heard the Crafty Cobbler is going out of business, too," said the shoemaker. "Our luck really has changed. I just hope the magic holds."

"Do you really think it is magic?" said Clara.

"I've no idea," said the shoemaker, "but I think it's finally time to find out."

*   *   *

That evening, instead of going upstairs to bed, Clara and the shoemaker left a candle burning on the workbench. Then they hid behind a curtain in the workshop and waited to see what would happen.

Just before midnight, the door creaked slowly open and two tiny figures darted across the floor and climbed up onto the workbench.

"Elves!" whispered Clara.

"Shhhhhhh!" said the shoemaker.

The couple watched in silence while the little people set to work on the huge heap of leather pieces. As their tiny needles

flew in and out, the elves chatted happily in their high-pitched, clickety language.

For hour after hour they worked tirelessly, stitching shoe after shoe after shoe. They hammered on heels, stuck on soles and fastened on buckles and bows, never once stopping to rest.

"Snikkety bakkity!" said one elf, admiring his final shoe. "Snokkety doo!" said the other, pointing to his own.

Just as the sun was rising, the elves jumped down from the bench and scampered out of the door.

"Mystery solved!" said the shoemaker, when they had gone. "But did you see the state of them?" said Clara. "Their clothes were all patched and frayed and they had no shoes on their little feet. They must be freezing."

"Poor wee things," said the shoemaker. "After all the help they have given us, I wish we could help *them* in some way."

"I have an idea . . . " said Clara.

All that day, even though they had had no sleep, the shoemaker and his wife worked. When she wasn't serving customers, Clara stitched clothes for the elves. She made two tiny jackets, two teeny waistcoats, two neat little shirts and two pointed elfin hats.

The shoemaker, instead of cutting out leather for new shoes, made miniature elf boots from the softest leather he could find and decorated them with tiny gold buttons.

"I hope they come back," said Clara.

"And I hope these fit," said her husband anxiously, displaying the teeny boots on the tips of his little fingers.

That night, the shoemaker and his wife left the clothes and boots on the workbench and hid behind the curtain again, waiting for the elves to appear.

Just before midnight, the door creaked open. The elves scurried in and clambered quickly up onto the workbench. As soon as they saw the clothes, they started jumping up and down and squealing and laughing in delight.

"Snappety, snappety sneeeeee!" squealed one.

"Kekkity, krakkety KOOOOO!" cried the other.

"I think they like them," whispered Clara, tears of happiness streaming down her cheeks.

The elves wasted no time in throwing off their rags and pulling on the tiny jackets, shirts and waistcoats. The shoemaker held his breath as they started to inspect the boots.

"Snikkety bakkity!" said one, admiring the tiny stitches.

"Snokkety doo!" said the other, pointing to the gold buttons.

The elves sat down to pull the boots onto their little feet. The shoemaker gave a silent sigh of relief. The boots were a perfect fit! Now the elves were dancing in delight, jigging across the workbench, jumping down to the floor and singing, at last in a language the shoemaker and his wife could understand:

"Now we are boys so fine to see,
No longer cobblers we will be!"

The excited elves danced, skipped and sang their way across the floor, out of the door, down the street and into the night, never to be seen again.

But that wasn't quite the end of the story. Even though their little helpers had gone, Clara and the shoemaker kept making and selling beautiful shoes. All their old customers returned, along with plenty of new ones, so the couple lived happily and comfortably for the rest of their lives.

And what about the Crafty Cobbler? He was last seen leaving town one dismal day, squelching through muddy puddles and muttering miserably as his shoddy shoes let in all the water.

JACK AND THE BEANSTALK

There was once a poor widow who had an only son named Jack, and an old cow whose name was Bluebell. For many years Jack and his mother just managed to make a living by selling Bluebell's milk at the market. But one morning Bluebell gave them no milk and they had nothing else to sell.

"What on earth shall we do now?" sobbed Jack's mother, staring into the empty milk pail.

"Oh, don't worry, mother," said Jack as cheerfully as he could. "I'm sure I can get a job or something. We'll be alright."

"But you've tried that before," said his mother. "And you know there's no work around here. We'll just have to sell Bluebell at the market and use the money to start a little shop."

Sadly, Jack agreed. It was the only thing they could do. He took the old cow's halter in his hand and led her slowly along the lane towards the market.

"Make sure you get a good price for her," called his mother.

Jack hadn't gone far when he met a funny-looking old man wearing a long, green cloak.

"Good morning, Jack," said the man.

"Good morning," said Jack, surprised that the stranger knew his name.

"And where are you off to this fine morning?" asked the man.

"Just off to market to sell our cow," said Jack.

"Well you look like the right sort of young man to sell a cow for a good price," said the man. "I expect you know how many beans makes five!"

"I do," said Jack. "Two in each hand and one in your mouth!"

"Indeed," chuckled the man, holding out his hand. "And here are those five beans. As you're so clever, you won't mind exchanging your cow for them, will you?"

"Doesn't seem like a very good idea," said Jack peering at the five small beans nestling in the man's cupped hand. "I think I'd better see how things go at the market."

"Oh, but you don't understand," said the old man, stepping into the path in front of Jack to bar his way. "You see, these are magic beans! If you plant them in the evening, by morning they can grow right up past the clouds and into the sky!"

"Really?" said Jack.

"Really," said the man.

"And if I'm not telling the truth, you can have your cow back."

Without thinking twice, Jack handed Bluebell over, pocketed the beans and ran back home.

There he saw his mother waiting by the gate.

"Did you get a good price?" she called when she saw her son returning without Bluebell.

"Oh yes!" called Jack brightly. "You'll never guess!"

"Five pounds?" said his mother with a big grin on her face.

"No!" said Jack.

"Ten pounds?" laughed his mother.

"No," said Jack.

"It can't be twenty!" squealed his mother, jumping up and down in delight.

"No," said Jack. "I got these!" And he held out his hand so his mother could see the five beans.

She just stared at his open hand in bewilderment.

"They're magic!" explained Jack. "You see, you plant them in the evening, and in the morning–"

"WHAT!" shrieked his mother. "What have you done,

you foolish boy? You have given away our cow for five shrivelled-up beans. You must be crazy!"

"These," she shouted, grabbing the beans from his hand, "are completely WORTHLESS!" And she threw the beans onto the ground in disgust.

"B-b-b-but—" mumbled Jack.

"No buts!" yelled his mother. "Just go straight to bed. There's nothing to eat, and I can't believe what you've done."

Jack scurried into the house and up to his little room where he threw himself down on the bed and cried himself to sleep.

* * *

When Jack woke up, his room was still dark.

"It must be very early," he thought, "and the sun's not up." But when he went over to the window and looked out, he could hardly believe his eyes.

The outside of the window was almost covered by the biggest, thickest, greenest leaves he had ever seen in his life.

The beans his mother had tossed so furiously onto the ground had grown overnight into an enormous beanstalk that reached up into the sky. It was just as the old man had said!

Jack wasted no time. He threw on his clothes, forced open the window, eased himself out through the leaves and grabbed hold of the huge stalk. Then he started to climb up, hand over hand, leaf by leaf.

He climbed and he climbed and he climbed. Up past the tallest trees, up past flocks of surprised birds, up through layer after layer of cloud and on and on into the sky.

When, at last, puffing and panting for breath, he reached the very top, he saw a long, white road stretching far into the distance.

Jack marched quickly along the road until he saw a massive house reaching even further into the sky. On the doorstep stood an immensely tall woman.

"Hello," called Jack politely. "I don't suppose you'd be so kind as to give me some breakfast? You see I haven't eaten for–"

"You'll be breakfast in a minute!" barked the woman. "My husband eats boys like you on toast. You'd better get going before he catches you. He'll be down any moment!"

"Oh, please, just a little piece of bread?" pleaded Jack. "I really am starving."

"Quickly then!" said the tall woman, taking pity on him. "I'll see what I can find." And she hurried him through the door, down an enormous echoing passageway and into the cavernous kitchen. There she lifted him onto the edge of the table and gave him a huge hunk of bread and a piece of cheese.

Jack was hungrily gobbling down the food when he heard a thunderous pounding noise coming from above. The plates on the dresser rattled as the whole house shook.

'THUD, THUD, THUD!'

"Oh no! It's my old man," whispered the woman.
"Quick, you must hide."

She picked Jack up and bundled him into the oven. At the
same moment a huge, hairy giant strode into the room chanting,

"FEE FI FO FUM, I SMELL THE
BLOOD OF AN ENGLISHMAN.
BE HE ALIVE OR BE HE DEAD,
I'LL GRIND HIS BONES
TO MAKE MY BREAD."

"I smell BOY!" roared the giant. "Is it fresh boy for breakfast?"

"Oh no, no, dear," said the giant's wife. "I haven't made your breakfast yet. Maybe you can smell the leftovers from yesterday – that boy you enjoyed so much for your supper? Why don't you go and have a shave? By the time you come back, I'll have your breakfast ready."

So the giant thudded out of the kitchen and back upstairs.

Jack was about to climb out of the oven and escape, when the woman said in a loud whisper:

"No, don't go! It's not safe yet. Wait till after he's had his breakfast. Then he has a nap and you can sneak out."

A few minutes later the giant thumped his way back into the kitchen and devoured an enormous breakfast.

Then he called to his wife:

"Can you bring me my little brown hen? You know the one that lays the special eggs?"

"Of course, dear," said his wife.

Jack peered through a crack, watching carefully as the giant took the little brown hen lovingly from his wife's hands and set it down gently on the table.

"Lay, lay, lay, little hen," cooed the giant, tenderly stroking the hen's back. The hen squawked loudly and ruffled her feathers.

Jack watched in amazement as a glistening golden egg rolled across the table. The giant reached out, grabbed the egg and thrust it deep into his pocket. Then he made himself comfortable in his chair by the fire and was soon snoring so loudly the whole house started shaking again.

Seeing his chance to escape, Jack jumped out of the oven, snatched up the hen, raced out of the door and hared out of the house. But then he heard a familiar noise behind him.

'THUD, THUD, THUD!'

The giant had woken up.

"WHERE'S MY HEN?" he bellowed as he lumbered out of the door and thundered along the road after Jack.

"FEE FI FO FUM,
I SMELL THE BLOOD OF AN ENGLISHMAN.
BE HE ALIVE OR BE HE DEAD,
I'LL GRIND HIS BONES TO MAKE MY BREAD."

The giant's booming chant was ringing in Jack's ears when he reached the top of the beanstalk. He leaped onto the nearest leaf and clambered down as fast as he could with the hen under his arm.

Down and down and down he climbed. But when he reached the top of the clouds, the beanstalk began to shake and sway. The giant was climbing down after him.

Faster and faster Jack climbed.
Closer and closer came the giant.

Now Jack was nearly level with the treetops.
"MOTHER! MOTHER!" he yelled. "Get the hatchet!"

Jack's mother came rushing out clutching their old hatchet. She screamed in terror when she saw one of the giant's enormous hairy hands emerging from the clouds.

Jack jumped to the ground, thrust the hen into his mother's hands, seized the tool and started to chop wildly at the beanstalk.

'CHOP CHOP CHOP,'
went Jack.

'THUD, THUD, THUD!'
went the giant.

Jack swung his arms high in the air and gave the beanstalk one last enormous chop. The giant felt the beanstalk quiver as it began to topple over.

'CRA-A-A-A-A-A-SH!'

The huge beanstalk and the giant clinging to it smashed onto the ground.

And that was the end of that fearsome old giant.

But for Jack and his mother it was a brand new start. The little brown hen was the answer to their prayers. All they had to do was to say, "Lay, lay, lay, little hen!" and they had a gleaming golden egg to sell.

With the money from selling the eggs, they bought a herd of cows, a flock of sheep, a fine young horse, some stylish new clothes and as much food as they needed. They lived happily in their cottage for many years.

And they were never bothered by boy-eating giants again.

ABOUT THE STORIES

Most of the tales in this book are traditional folk stories which may have been passed down from generation to generation for centuries before they were ever written down.

Although we can't always know exactly where the stories first came from, it is still often possible to trace when they were first written down, and to see how they were gradually shaped into the tales we enjoy today.

STONE SOUP

This is an ancient European and Scandinavian folk tale and there are many different versions, such as 'Nail Soup' and 'Button Soup'. It was probably first written down over two hundred years ago. In France and Hungary, the old man is replaced by a group of soldiers; in Portugal he is always a monk. The story is usually told to demonstrate the benefits of working together, especially in times of great hardship and scarcity.

THE GINGERBREAD MAN

This was first written down in 1875 in the American magazine 'St. Nicholas', where it was called 'The Gingerbread Boy'. Before this, the story was already popular and may have been inspired by stories about a runaway pancake written in Germany over a hundred and fifty years ago. Many writers have added to the story over the years and introduced characters such as the cunning fox.

THE PRINCESS AND THE PEA

This tale was written over a hundred and fifty years ago by Danish author Hans Christian Andersen. He heard the story as a child, but it is thought to come originally from Sweden. Similar stories can be found in other countries such as Italy and India, so it existed for very many years before Andersen made it famous.

THE BOY WHO CRIED WOLF and THE HARE AND THE TORTOISE

These are both Aesop's Fables, which are a group of stories first told over two thousand years ago in Ancient Greece and shared all over the world ever since. Each fable has a moral, or a lesson at the end. Although his stories are so well known, no one really knows who Aesop was. Some say he was a slave whose clever tales eventually won him his freedom and the approval of the king.

GOLDILOCKS AND THE THREE BEARS

This is based on 'The Story of the Three Bears' written by English author Robert Southey over a hundred and fifty years ago. For a long time people thought he'd made the story up, but then it was discovered that a woman named Eleanor Mure had written a poem about the three bears, based on a story from folklore. The version that she knew wasn't quite the same as the story retold today. Instead of Goldilocks, there was an old woman in the story, but after some years she was replaced by a little girl called Silver Hair. After that, the little girl was given different names, such as Silver-Locks and Golden Hair. It wasn't until a hundred years ago that Goldilocks finally got her name.

LITTLE RED RIDING HOOD

This is based on a French story written over three hundred years ago by Charles Perrault. Folk tales from France, Austria, and Italy gave Perrault the inspiration, but the origins of 'Little Red Riding Hood' can be traced back much further.

Two thousand years ago, a folk tale about a wolf who dresses up as a nanny goat to eat the goat's kids was first told in Europe and the Middle East. A thousand years later, a new version of this story emerged in which the goat was replaced with a grandmother. However, it would be another six hundred years before Charles

Perrault wrote his version, at about the same time
as a Chinese poet named Huang Zhing recorded the
Chinese version of the story. A popular tale throughout
history and across the world, 'Little Red Riding Hood' has
since been rewritten many times, including by the Brothers Grimm
two hundred years ago.

THE GOLDEN FISH

This comes from a Russian story in verse called 'The Tale of
the Fisherman and the Fish', written over a hundred and fifty
years ago by the famous Russian poet Alexander Pushkin.

Pushkin was inspired by a story by the two
German writers Jacob and Wilhelm Grimm
(known as the Brothers Grimm) which they
called 'The Fisherman and his Wife'. The
brothers began collecting and retelling
traditional fairytales in 1806 and published
many collections. This story came
from the painter Philipp Otto
Runge, who had written
it down for a
folk poetry
collection.

The Elves and the Shoemaker

This tale was written two hundred years ago as part of one of Jacob and Wilhelm Grimm's collections of traditional German folk tales. The Brothers Grimm had loved the stories they heard as young boys, and decided to write down as many as possible. They asked friends and family to recount the stories they knew, and listened to as many storytellers as they could find. This story comes from Dorothea (also known as Dortchen) Wild, the brothers' childhood friend who became Wilhelm's wife in 1825.

Jack and the Beanstalk

This story is based on a popular English folk tale first written down by Benjamin Tabart over two hundred years ago. It is thought to have its roots in Viking myth and legend. Another Englishman named Joseph Jacobs rewrote the story in 'English Fairy Tales' published in 1890, but by that time it was already a popular pantomime story. The giant's traditional cry of "fee fi fo fum" dates back at least as far as 1605.

It is Joseph Jacobs' version that is most often retold today and this is believed to be closer to the original folk story. 'Jack and the Beanstalk' is an unusual nursery tale because the hero does not marry at the end but returns to his mother.

Designed by Nicola Butler

Additional design work by John Russell and Keith Newell

Cover design by Keith Newell

Editorial assistance: Alice Beecham and Alice Primmer